D0970720

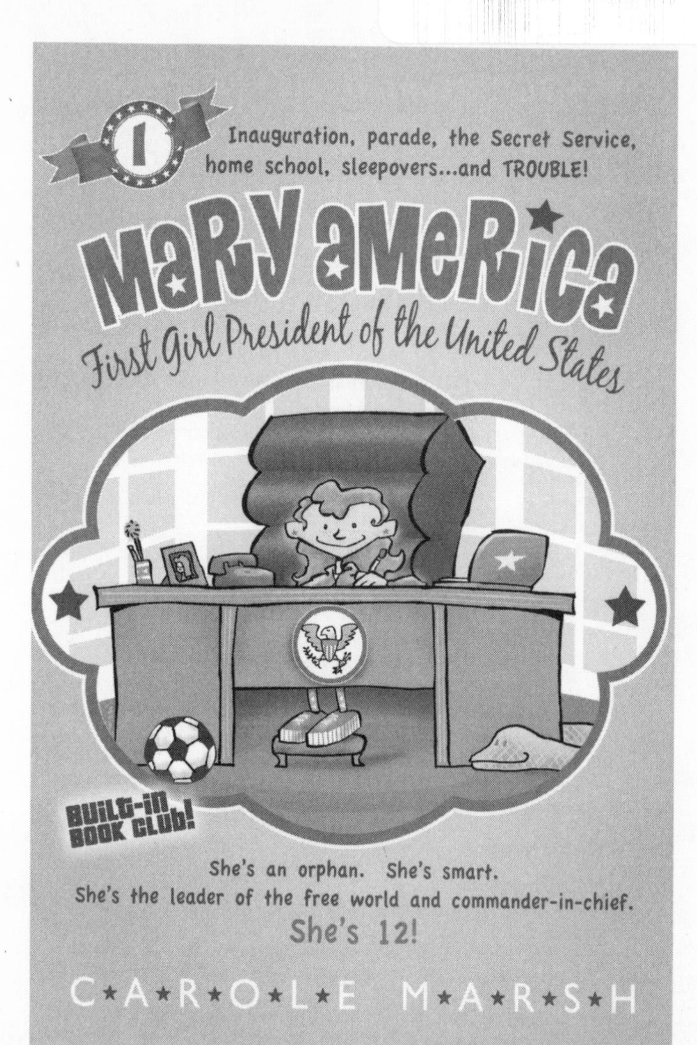
1
Inauguration, parade, the Secret Service, home school, sleepovers...and TROUBLE!
Mary America
First Girl President of the United States
BUILT-IN BOOK CLUB!
She's an orphan. She's smart.
She's the leader of the free world and commander-in-chief.
She's 12!
C★A★R★O★L★E M★A★R★S★H

Second Printing, July 2011

Published by Gallopade International/Carole Marsh Books.
Printed in the United States of America.

Managing Editor: Sherry Moss
Senior Editor: Janice Baker
Cover / Content Design: Vicki DeJoy
Cover / Content Illustration: John Kovaleski

For Christina, Grant, Avery, Ella, Evan,
and all other boys and girls who dream
of growing up and becoming president
one day—study hard!

Other Books by Carole Marsh

The White House Christmas Mystery
The Counterfeit Constitution Mystery

Leader of the free world, commander-in-chief, and handling a crisis in the Situation Room... with the help of her friends!

War and peace, red tape, funny money, Air Force One...and Disney World diplomacy!

Mary America

First Girl President of the United States

by Carole Marsh

Prologue

IT WAS STRANGE how it happened. Millard Standish Willoughby was elected president of the United States. His wife had died ten years earlier of cancer. Their oldest daughter, Abigail, had been a lawyer. She had married another lawyer, Joseph America. While on assignment in a war zone for the U.S. military, they had both been killed in a bomb attack on a courthouse.

And so when President Willoughby took office and came to live in the White House, he brought his two orphaned grandchildren, Mary and Josh, with him.

President Willoughby adored them both, but was especially fond of the oldest, Mary.

She had her mother's beautiful skin, eyes, and hair, and she was smart. She had already skipped several grades in school, and was eligible to go on to college. Instead, Mary held the Bible while her grandfather took the oath of office, marched down Pennsylvania Avenue on a blue-sky, winter's day in the Inauguration parade, and settled into the White House at her grandfather's side.

During his first two years of office, President Willoughby had been exceedingly effective. He was decisive, popular, a good man at getting people on opposite sides of the fence to listen, learn, and, even if gritting their teeth, agree. It was hard to pinpoint exactly when his health began to fail. Like former president Franklin D. Roosevelt, who suffered from polio, the folks who surrounded him helped cover up President Willoughby's almost imperceptible, but growing, disabilities.

At first it was just a little forgetfulness. But slowly things grew worse. An energetic man, he began to need frequent "catnaps" to get through the day. Almost no one outside of his immediate circle of aides, closest friends, the White House physician, and his granddaughter, of course, realized that the robust man had changed.

On the surface, the White House and the world went on, President Willoughby always there to give press conferences, meet with heads of state, kick-off the annual Easter Egg Roll, and other presidential duties, slight and serious.

As always, Mary, nicknamed by the media the "Little First Lady" (a term she did not care for), was nearby. She spent time in the Oval Office, attended many meetings, and "to witness history," as her grandfather put it, could even be found in the tense Situation Room of the White House during a crisis.

On November 21, precisely at midnight, President Millard Standish Willoughby had a heart attack and died. In the hours that followed, it was discovered that after a former law had been changed to allow a certain California governor to run for president (in spite of not being a native-born American), a minor, but dramatic, alteration had subsequently been made and signed into law by President Willoughby. This clause changed the requirements related to the age limits for presidential eligibility. Indeed, any age limits at all had been removed.

The new stipulation specified no age, but that the candidate must have an IQ of at least 140. Another law had been added specifying that if a president could not finish his term, he could name a successor to finish that term. At 11:59 p.m. on the night of November 21, President Willoughby, White House lawyer at

his side, had inked in his choice. The document had been notarized.

At 1:17 a.m. on November 22, Mary America, IQ 146, had been sworn in as the new President of the United States. The Bible she swore the oath on had rested on her deceased grandfather's chest. As required, Mary completed the oath by saying in a quiet, but assured voice: "I do solemnly swear." She then bent over and kissed her beloved grandfather goodbye on his forehead. She thus became the new commander-in-chief and leader of the free world.

President Mary America was twelve years old.

Five months later...
Monday, 9:00 a.m.
The Oval Office

BECAUSE HER FEET would not reach the floor, a small footstool had been placed beneath the presidential desk in the Oval Office for Mary America to rest her feet on. Whenever she sat at her desk (one that had once belonged to President Franklin D. Roosevelt), she always peeked beneath first to see if either "Ssss," her big, green boa constrictor, or Josh, her pesky younger brother, were hiding there.

The reason she had to check was that Josh would often sneak down there while Mary was doing some presidential concentrating and tie her shoe- laces together so that when she tried to stand up, she tripped. And Ssss had learned how

to untie her shoelaces, so when she tried to stand up, she also got entangled and tripped.

Mary did not like to trip up. She took being President very seriously. It was a hard job. Being smart made it easier. Being a kid made it harder. People often thought they could "trip Mary up" because she was just twelve years old, but they soon learned better.

Nonetheless, it did not help a President to fall flat on her face when greeting the Secretary of State or the Queen of England. So Mary always checked her shoes—twice.

This morning, Josh was at school. He was lucky that he got to go to public school, Mary thought. Her other grandfather (referred to as the First Gramps by the media), who lived with them in the White House, had insisted that Josh not be escorted by the Secret Service to school.

Josh was disappointed, but it was not like Gramps to be foiled in any plan. (He and Mary had that in common.) Their grandfather had insisted that the school bus pick Josh up each morning and bring him back each afternoon. So everyday, the big yellow bus had to stop for Bomb Check. The school bus driver, short, little, bald Mr. Crumbly had to show his ID. And ALL the kids squealed greetings to Josh, who waited patiently beneath the north portico to get picked up.

Mary was always a little wistful as she watched the cheery school bus motor off. Mr. Crumbly always gave her a "high five" out his window as he pulled away and the joyful cheers faded as the bus left the White House gates.

Due to "security issues," Mary was home schooled. At least she was home schooled in the White House. She preferred to say she was "house

schooled," but Gramps said that made it sound like she had a building for a teacher.

In a way, she sort of did. The White House was certainly a constant education, she thought, as she doodled on her President of the United States of America notepad. But this morning, Mary's job was to educate Congress, which did not seem to be able to balance its budget.

"Got it all figured out?" asked Mrs. Denim, her former fourth grade teacher, who now served as the Secretary to the President. That had been Gramps' idea, too. He thought it would add some stability to his granddaughter's day to have a friendly, familiar face nearby, and it was. But even better, Mrs. Denim was really, really "teacher good" at dismissing people who just thought they could barge or charm their way in to see the President whenever they wished.

Also, Mrs. Denim made great hot chocolate, which she placed on a Presidential Seal coaster at Mary's right hand each morning promptly at 9:30.

"Thank you, Mrs. Denim," Mary said. She sipped a quick, careful gulp, and as always, wound up with a whipped cream moustache.

"Charming, Miss President," Mrs. Denim said. "That makes you look like the elder senator from the great state of Vermont."

Mary giggled. With a deft swipe of her tongue she swept the cream away. "I just wish these senators and Congressmen and women could add! I know there are a lot of zeroes in a budget, but really, as near as I can tell one minus two is still a negative number. I learned that in kindergarten. Didn't they?"

Mrs. Denim sighed. "You'd think. I do believe I had a couple of these folks in my class

way back when. I don't recall that math was their best subject. So a lot of red ink?"

"Red as blood!" Mary complained. "And I have to go before Congress tomorrow and I am sure they want me to approve their big, bad budget, but I just can't do it." Mary stomped her right foot on her footstool for emphasis and felt a big *SQUASH*. She looked. Yep, Ssss had taken up residence there, napping as usual. She gave her sweet, silly pet a foot rub. If he slept, maybe he wouldn't slither up the side of her desk and sneak cocoa like he often did. Usually the whipped cream ended up on the top of his head like a pioneer lady's bonnet.

"Soooooooo?" inquired Mrs. Denim, removing the empty cocoa mug and wiping up peanut butter cookie crumbs.

"So I have to think of an idea," Mary said, sighing. "I don't mind one bit telling Congress,

'Thanks, but no thanks,' on behalf of the American people who DO have to balance their budgets. But I want to give them an idea to help them out."

As Mrs. Denim walked across the Oval Office rug filled with the Presidential Seal she asked, "So you'll do what you always do when you have a Congressional conundrum?"

Mary grinned. "You bet!"

"Call in the Kitchen Cabinet?" Mrs. Denim asked.

"Yes!" said Mary. "Please email them all and tell them to bring their..."

"Their calculators?" Mrs. Denim guessed.

Mary shook her red curls. "No," she said. "Ask them to bring, hmm...glitter, glue sticks, and, you know, felt and sequins and other crafty stuff."

Mrs. Denim looked utterly puzzled. "TOP SECRET?" I assume.

Mary sat up very straight in her most presidential pose. "Oh, absolutely TOP SECRET, Mrs. Denim. Absolutely TOP SECRET!"

Monday, 10:30 a.m.
The Oval Office

THE OVAL OFFICE is in the West Wing of the White House. It is the President's official and formal office. It is, well, it's oval in shape. The walls swoop around the room in a soft curve. Even the windows that look out onto a grove of trees are curved. Where the walls curve, there are doors you can see. But there are also doors that you can't really see until someone pushes on the "wall" and a hidden panel opens.

The White House is full of secret doors and stairways and other shortcuts to help those

who have permission move from place to place. Every morning at 10:30 sharp, Mary's Chief of Staff slipped through one of the buttercream frosting-colored panels and sat in one of the armchairs across from Mary's desk. It was time to do business.

"Good morning, Mary," the COS said. "How are you?" He looked down and frowned and scooted his chair back a foot or two. "And how's Ssss?"

Mary looked up. "I'm fine and Ssss…(she cocked her head to listen)…I believe Ssss is snoring."

The COS exhaled. "Good. Shall we begin?" He did not wait for an answer but steadily breezed through the day's agenda, calendar, reports, news updates, and "situations," if there were any. There almost always were.

"Let's see," the COS began: "You have a light day because of your trip to Capitol Hill tomorrow. I've canceled any frou-frou stuff like greeting visiting schoolchildren..."

"But I *love* to see the school kids who come to visit the White House on field trips!" Mary said. "At least *they* seem happy to see me...and *they* smile."

The COS looked up. He did not smile. "Friday, I'll give you all the noisy, smelly, little school rats you can handle," he said. "Ok?"

Mary had the power to override her Chief of Staff, but she knew he was just trying to help her manage her ever-busy days. "Ok."

The COS continued. He reeled off a dizzying list of "*Meet with...Call...Greet...Just a few minutes with...And also...And don't forget...And if there is time we need to slip in...Oh, and also Mrs...and...*"

The list went on and on and on. Mary knew she did not need to remember it or write it down. There were aides to remind her of everything except when to go to the bathroom! Sometimes she thought being president was sort of like when she used to play Little League—receiving a constant series of surprise pitches when she was at bat. You never knew what was next, but you had to be prepared and respond, or get caught with a ball in your head or belly or kneecap, or get "struck out." Well, really, no one could strike her out here, at least not for three more years when she came up for reelection.

When Mary looked up from her doodling, she saw that the COS had slipped back out of the Oval Office. Mary wiggled her right foot; she looked down. Sure enough, Ssss had disappeared.

"One-thousand-one...one-thousand-two...one-thousand-three..." Just as she expected, she heard a scream. Ssss had followed the COS out yet again. "Serves him right," Mary said aloud to herself. "Next time he won't nix the school kids!"

Behind her a gentle voice said, "Serve you right, that's vhat I vant to do!"

The White House chef had entered the office from another door for his weekly appointment. When Mary nodded, he took a seat. "Your culinary vish is my command!" Chef said. "What'll it be this veek, Miss President?"

No matter how hard Mary had tried, she could not even get her closest personal staff to just call her Mary. When she had first taken office and asked, they would just nod and smile, and continue to address her as Miss President.

However, when a blustery Congressman had had the audacity to call her "Mary" in an early meeting in the Oval Office, everyone in the room had gasped in shock and discomfort. The man had immediately apologized.

"Now, Chef," Mary teased. She loved the big, white-headed man in his big, white chef pants and shirt and crooked toque that sat on his head like a lopsided soufflé. "Let's have all vegetables all week like turnips and rutabagas and squash, and no dessert at all whatsoever, please."

Chef shook his head. "Miss President, you teash Chef so! I know it is: waffles for breakfash...PB&J for lunsh...and whatever your Grampsh wants for dinner...and let Miss Doodah cook for baby Priscilla as she prefersh, correct?"

Mary sat with her arms folded listening to Chef's lilting accented litany. "Correct. *And...*"

"And," Chef continued, "re-stock the candy jars, popcorn bin, cookie jar, and (he whispered) your secret stash of certain spechial foods your Grampsh does not know exists."

"Perfect!" said Mary. "But I also need a special dish for tomorrow afternoon, please."

Mary scribbled on her notepad and turned it around. "And a very sharp knife," Mary added with a secretive wink.

Chef picked up the note and chewed on his lip as he read the surprising request. At first he looked puzzled, then his face brightened. He snapped his fat fingers. "Aha! Got it!" He put a finger to his lips. "And shhhhhh's the word!"

"Uh, mum's the word," Mary said.

"You want flowersh?" Chef asked, befuddled.

"No, Chef," Mary said and smiled. "Just the special dish."

In a light puff of baking powder, Chef bowed and disappeared out the windowed door.

Monday, 10:45 a.m.
The Oval Office

STORM CLOUDS PUSHED gray shadows across the Oval Office. Mary shivered and tugged her hoodie closer around her neck. She felt an even darker shadow stalk silently into the room behind her.

"It's time," said a deep voice.

Mary turned. "Oh, hi, Todd."

Todd was Mary's Secret Service agent. She actually had lots of them. LOTS. But Todd was her personal one who pretty much followed her everywhere but the bathroom. At first, she thought having a Secret Service agent was a big bore and an insult to her inalienable right to

privacy. But now, she and Todd were best friends—not that you'd know. The Secret Service had a lot of rules, but sometimes, in spite of the bulge of gun beneath his black jacket and the curlicue of silly black phone cord behind his ear, Mary could get Todd to crack a smile.

"I have a great idea," Mary said, standing up and stretching. "Why don't you go today and let me stay here and watch television?"

Today was one of Todd's smile days. "Yes, I am certain that no one would notice that a very large black man in a black suit with big, black running shoes, a gun bulge, and a headset has taken your place."

Mary giggled. "Really, Todd, you might be surprised."

But Todd had turned serious, as anyone in charge of the protection—indeed the life—of the

President of the United States—would be. After checking the corridor, he motioned for Mary to follow him.

All but invisible behind the very large man, Mary silently followed the agent as he very rapidly made his way down a number of hallways and around several corners and up a short set of stairs. Sometimes Mary had to add a little skip step to keep up. Along the way, if they met anyone, that person would stop, nod, and mutter, "Morning, Miss President."

Mary nodded back, but mostly she quick-stepped until they came to a doorway and Todd stepped aside to let her enter.

"Good luck," he always said softly, as he backed out of the doorway.

"Easy for you to say," Mary always responded, but usually Todd had already resumed

SCHOOL

his Secret Service position face-out by the door with his stern "I'm guarding" look.

However, as soon as Mary entered the cheerful room, Ms. Tendril always immediately glanced up and smiled a glistening smile.

"Good morning, Mary!" she said cheerfully. "Please take your seat."

Mary did and so her daily hour of home school began. There had been some discussion about whether Mary, with her high IQ, needed school at all. After all, she had already completed high school by age 10 and most of a college degree by age 12, when her education had been interrupted by her grandfather's death and her being named President of the United States.

It had been Mary (with only a brief doubt) who had insisted that she continue her schooling while in office. "Gramps always says learning is for life," she said, "so it does seem I'm a little young to stop learning. Besides, there's always something new under the sun to learn."

Mary did not confess that she secretly wanted to be an astronomer and an archaeologist after she had finished being President. Since she did not know if she'd be re-elected for another term, she had no idea how soon that would be. Who knew: maybe she'd even grow up and get married and have kids one day.

Mary wasn't so sure about that. Living in the White House with her and Gramps and Josh and Ssss were her Aunt Doodah, her mother's younger sister, and Aunt Doodah's baby, Priscilla. Since baby Prissy, as they all called her, was a crawler on the verge of toddling, she was a handful. But it was Aunt Doodah who was really the handful! If there was an Uncle Doodah, Mary had never met him.

Anyway, a future career was in the future. It was time for school. Mary missed going to school with her friends, but at least she could look forward to seeing them later this afternoon for their Kitchen Cabinet meeting and weekly Monday night sleepover. She could hardly wait.

Ms. Tendril was patiently waiting for Mary to focus. Usually there was a specific class study scheduled, but if Mary wanted to study something else, like where Azerbaijan was, or the history of world diplomacy, or how a nuclear bomb was built, Ms. Tendril was always ready to accommodate her.

The classroom was small but filled wall-to-wall from floor to ceiling with a fabulous library. The latest computers, hard drives, monitors, and other tech gear, including a small chemistry lab, completed the room. The only thing the room didn't have was a window.

"I think today, I'd like to study economics," Mary told Ms. Tendril, who did not look a bit surprised by the request.

Ms. Tendril picked up a fancy, high-tech calculator.

"Oh, not that kind of economics," Mary said. She slid an Office of the President notepad close to her and picked up one of a dozen pinpoint-sharpened White House pencils. "A little more basic. I just want to see if, for example, 2 minus 1 still equals 1. Or, maybe, if 5 minus ten still equals minus-5."

For a moment, Ms. Tendril looked puzzled. Then she shook her blond curls knowingly. "Hmm, headed to Capitol Hill tomorrow, are you? I understand perfectly!"

And so for the next hour, without even a break, Mary and her teacher did math: little math, big math, hard math. And by the end of the

class, Mary could see that just as she had expected, 2 plus 2 still did equal 4 and not 4 million, or anywhere close.

Mary was smart, but she also liked to be absolutely sure that she was absolutely right—especially when she had to deal with adults wearing suits. Especially when she had to stand up before lots of them and know exactly what she was talking about.

Exactly.

Monday, noon
The Residence

AFTER SCHOOL, TODD escorted Mary to the family dining room. As always, he immediately vanished, although Mary was sure she'd heard his stomach growl. Of course, her own tummy was rumbling pretty loudly, too.

"Hi, Sweetie Pie!" Gramps called as Mary came into the room. It was nice to hear someone refer to her other than Miss President.

"Hi, Gramps!" Mary said, running into her grandfather's arms and giving him a fat kiss on his pink cheek. His white sideburns tickled her nose.

"How was school?" asked Gramps, as they sat down at the table.

"Enlightening!" said Mary, drinking a big gulp of milk.

"Oh, so you're studying Thomas Edison?" teased her grandfather.

Mary giggled. "No. More like Adam Smith."

Gramps pretended to be confused. "You mean the man who wore a fig leaf?" he said, slamming his hands to his cheeks and pretending to be embarrassed.

"No, silly," Mary said with a laugh.

"Oh," said Gramps, "then you must mean that Smith guy, the one who hung around with Pocahontas?"

Mary doubled over with giggles. She loved her silly, old grandfather. The media tried to make Gramps seem old and senile, but really he was very smart, and quite handsome, she thought. And ever so kind. His only goal seemed to make Mary's job as President as easy as possible. She knew he had not been in favor of her taking on such a role at such a young age, but he had let her decide.

"Gramps, who's the boss around here?" asked Mary, another game they always played.

Her grandfather stared at the ceiling as if thinking hard about the question, "Uhhhhhhh, me?"

"No!" said Mary, knowing that in The Residence he was indeed the boss. "Me! And I'm giving you Direct Presidential Order Number 34796A."

"Which is?" asked Gramps.

"Eat your peanut butter and jelly right now!" said Mary.

"And what if I really prefer a salad?" Gramps asked, as Ms. Hightower, their server placed a yummy-looking Cobb salad before him.

Mary sighed and wagged a finger at her grandfather. "Then I grant you Presidential Pardon Number 12J9075—but just this one time, mind you."

Suddenly they were both distracted as Josh dashed into the room, hair, jacket, books, and papers flapping around him, then flying to the floor. He jumped into a chair and tackled the PB&J sandwich before him.

"What are you doing home so early?" Mary asked.

"Thudy wath urluh ghme duh," Josh mumbled.

"Huh?" said Gramps.

"He says today was early go home day," Mary translated. "I think they have tests next week. He's probably supposed to study this afternoon."

"I'm certain of that," teased Gramps. "Right after lunch."

"Absolutely," said Mary. "No pool or bowling or gym or basketball..."

Josh's mouth was so full he couldn't talk, so he just shook his head No-No-No back and forth rapidly.

Their friendly family banter was interrupted when Aunt Doodah bounded into the room, holding Prissy.

"Hi, Prez!" she said, dumping Prissy into the high chair. "Pesky brother," she added, snitching half of Josh's sandwich and giving it to her baby. "Old man," she said, giving Gramps a quick hug. She took a seat and stared at the sandwiches and the salad. "Isn't there any piiiiiiiizzzzzzza?" she moaned, like she always did.

Mary thought Aunt Doodah was an anomaly. She didn't seem to know if she actually wanted to be a grown-up mother or still act like a crazy college kid, even if she didn't go to college. She was ever so much fun, but Mary also thought she was really sad inside. Mary thought her aunt felt like an orphan too. While she had been grateful to come to live with them when Mary moved into the White House, Mary was pretty sure she wanted to be somewhere else, but just didn't know where or how or when.

"Jah...jah...jah..." squealed Prissy, trying to say Josh. Josh was her favorite person in the whole world, and right now he was making silly faces at her, which she loved. "JAH...JAH...JAH..."

Suddenly, there was another loud, yet muffled, squeal. Ms. Hightower just couldn't get used to the fact that most days, the family dining room door mysteriously opened by itself, or seemed to. Just a crack, mind you, but that was enough for Ssss to swish his way into the kitchen and up onto a chair. Ms. Hightower was mortally afraid of the snake, and you had to hope you had all your food because once Ssss made an appearance, Ms. Hightower vanished until Ssss did.

"SSSS...SSSSS...SSSSSSSSSS!" squealed Prissy, pretty much spitting slobbery peanut butter and jelly over them all.

Aunt Doodah huffed. "That..."

"Don't say a bad word," Gramps reminded her quickly, as Ssss returned to the dining room.

"...that doggone snake!" Aunt Doodah finished, politically-correctly.

Mary reached over and gave Ssss a pat and a piece of her own sandwich. Later, Todd would be sure the boa constrictor got something a bit more manly to eat.

"Who have you been terrorizing today, Ssss?" Gramps asked. "I hope that Democratic dimwit, Mr. Kn..."

"Now, Gramps," Mary sternly warned. "Let's not criticize the peoples' representatives in Washington, please."

"Yeah, Gramps," said Josh. "This joint could be bugged, you know!"

Josh had been on a class field trip to the Spy Museum downtown, and now saw spies

around every corner. Mary always assured him that was not the case, but actually, she wasn't quite sure of the truth, herself.

She and Josh still missed Mom and Dad and their other grandfather a lot. When they said "the President," it was often him they still meant. Sometimes Mary felt like they were in some kind of dream or maybe a Disney movie. She was too busy to be sad most of the time, and she tried to spend time with Josh. He was a pesky brother, but he was *her* pesky brother and she loved him dearly. Well, most of the time.

"Mary?" Gramps asked softly. "Is anything wrong?"

"Earth to Mary! Earth to Mary!" Josh hollered. "You were staring at the chandelier again, Sis."

Mary blushed.

"Aw, leave her alone," said Aunt Doodah. "The poor girl's got the woes of the world on her shoulders, you know." She picked up a yawning Prissy.

"Oh, it's not that bad," said Mary, absent-mindedly.

Aunt Doodah gave her a "You-gotta-be-kidding-me!" look. "Hey, kid, I was kidding. Prez—piece of cake."

"Speaking of cake," said Josh. "Isn't there any dessert today?"

"Ms. Hightower?" Gramps called toward the kitchen. "Ms. Hightower? Mary has to go back to work. The baby needs a nap. Josh has to study..."

Josh groaned and stuck out his tongue at his sister. From the kitchen, they heard a muffled reply.

"What did she say?" asked Aunt Doodah, who never ate dessert. She didn't want to ruin her perfect figure, she always said. She was pretty much a stick with sleeves.

"She said when Ssss leaves," said Josh.

Gramps hopped up. "I'll take care of this." Agilely, he pelted through the swinging door and back out. He held a platter of frosted brownies in his hand and passed them around. The clan cheered.

"Thanks, Gramps," said Mary, picking an extra one for Ssss.

Soon, she knew, Josh would be on the computer. Prissy would be sleeping in her pink crib in the nursery. Gramps would sit on the sun porch and read. And Aunt Doodah would, well, she would do whatever Aunt Doodah did when she disappeared, which was usually just about all the doodah day.

And Mary, well, Mary... There was Todd now. Mary wiped her mouth, blew kisses to them all and left the room to go back to work.

And Ssss? Oh, Ssss stayed behind...to help Ms. Hightower tidy-up.

Monday, 1:00 p.m.
The West Wing

SOON, MARY WAS busy in the West Wing. Her busy afternoon included:

- Meeting with the Secretary of State
- Greeting a Girl Scout troop from Iowa in the Rose Garden
- Catching up with the Secretary of Defense on some gnarly national security problems
- Writing a letter to the family of a soldier
- Making a call to the Prime Minister of Canada
- Approving a menu for the next State dinner
- Reading a few TOP SECRET/EYES ONLY reports
- Sitting briefly for the artist who would paint her official presidential portrait

But all that time, in the back of her mind, Mary kept thinking of her idea and wondering if it would work. She could hardly wait until time for her Kitchen Cabinet meeting.

Suddenly, Mary felt something tickle her foot. She smiled. Ssss, she thought.

When did that silly, old snake sneak in, she wondered. She wiggled her toes to say, "Hi."

The door opened slightly and Mrs. Denim gave Mary her daily wink that meant, "Time's up!" Mary smiled back at her and stretched. She'd been sitting at the big desk far too long.

As she scooted her feet off the footstool beneath and tried to stand up, she tripped face first into a pile of papers, stood right back up, then fell back into her chair.

"What is..." she began when she heard a giggle. "JOSH?!"

Her brother peeked out from under the Oval Office desk and grinned.

"How many times are you going to sneak down there and tie my shoelaces together?" Mary complained.

Josh laughed. "As long as you fall for it! Get it? FALL for it!"

"Oh, yeah, I get it, pesky brother! And I'm going to get you!" Mary grabbed for his tee shirt, but he was too quick for her.

"At least I didn't tie them in knots this time," Josh said, untying and retying his sister's shoelaces.

Mary sighed. "Well, thank you—I guess. I thought you were Ssss," she added.

Josh bellowed. "Oh, Mary, I wish you could have seen Ms. Hightower! She came in to clear the table and Ssss wrapped himself

around her ankles. She screamed bloody murder...it was soooooo funny!"

"Josh! That's not nice. Where were you, anyway?" asked Mary.

Josh shrugged his shoulders. "Hiding under the table, of course."

Mary grinned and shook her head. "You really would make a good spy, you know."

"I know!" said her brother proudly. "I've been practicing my invisible writing."

"Well, don't use it in *this* office!" Mary warned him. "Promise?"

Josh just smiled and ran out the door.

"JOSSSSSSSSH!" Mary called after him, but it was no use. He had vanished. As President, Mary had control over a lot of things—but her little brother was not one of them!

Monday, 3:00 p.m.
The White House swimming pool

THIS WAS MARY'S favorite time of the day. After so many hours of work and school, she loved her first dive into the White House swimming pool. She always tried to splash Todd, but he always stood just too far out of reach by a big potted palm.

The best part of this time of day was that Mary knew what came next, at least on Mondays, and it happened right now:

The double doors to the pool pavilion sprung open and all her best girlfriends in the world scampered in.

"Mary!" "Hi, Mary!" "We're changing, Mary!" "How do you always get down here first, Mary?" the girls said in turn. "Hi, Tooooooodd,"

one of the girls added and blew a kiss to the Secret Service agent who ignored her.

Mary smiled and waved. "Well, hurry up, I'm seven laps ahead of you!"

In a few minutes, her friends were in and out of the dressing room. They had exchanged their school uniforms and books for swimsuits and swim fins, or a beach ball, or a pink float, whatever they happened to grab.

Mico threw the float into the center of the pool and the girls all swam to it and held on. They had a little ritual that they went through that had started when Mary moved to the White House.

"Hi, I'm Mico," said a tiny girl with long dark hair and big dark eyes. "I'm 10 and I go to Sidwell Friends School, and I want to be a doctor when I grow up."

"Hi, Mico!" said the next girl in the circle around the float. "I'm J.J. and I'm 11 years old,

and I go to P.S. 97 and we're going to beat you in soccer!" Her blond curls bobbed in glistening wet ringlets around her head.

"Hi, J.J.," a girl with long brown braids said merrily. "My name is Beah and I'm 14…"

"NO WAY!" all the other girls cried, splashing Beah.

"No, really," said Beah, "I'm 12, and I home school, and I'm going to be in the annual, city spelling bee!"

"Beah in the bee!" the girls cried, splashing her once again.

"Hey, you guys, don't forget me!" said a pretty, dark-skinned girl. "As you well know, I am Kinta, and I am 11, and I just got picked for the Math Bowl at my school today!"

"Congratulations, Kinta!" all the girls cried. Then they all turned and looked at Mary, who groaned.

"Oh, all right," she said. "I'm Mary and I'm 12 and I go to school on the [she shoved her thumb upwards] third floor of the West Wing..."

"ANNNNNDDDDDDD?" the girls said.

"And I'm the President of the United States," Mary finished.

Now, all the girls did whoop and holler. They still couldn't get over that their best friend was President. But really, that wasn't what was important to them. They just liked having her for a friend. That's why they liked to tease her about her job.

"*Hiiiiiii, Mary!*" the girls all cheered.

For a while, the girls swam laps, played Marco/Polo, shoved one another off the side of the pool, and otherwise had a blast. Everything was going swimmingly, you could say, until...

"YIIIIIIIIIKES!"

"HELLLLLP!"

"GET ME OUTTA HERE!"

"RUN FOR YOUR LIVES!!!!!!!"

Ssss had slithered into the pool for his afternoon swim.

"It's just Ssss," Mary told them, "not the Loch Ness Monster." Her friends weren't really afraid of her pet boa constrictor, but they always made a big to-do when they found him in the pool.

Soon, the girls had dried off and changed clothes. They hauled all their backpacks and squeezed themselves into a secret elevator and Todd took them up to The Residence.

"Thank you," said Mico.

"Thanks," said J.J.

"Appreciate the ride," said Beah.

"*Thanks, Toooooooooodd,*" swooned Kinta.

The last one off the elevator, Mary turned to the agent and said, "You could take a break, you

know. We're just going to hang out and behave."

Todd, towering over Mary, looked down at her. "I don't think so, Miss President," he said. "Ya'll never do."

Monday, 4:15 p.m.
The Residence

THE GIRLS GATHERED on the sun porch, where Ms. Hightower had left a plate of chocolate chip cookies and a pitcher of pink lemonade.

"The Kitchen Cabinet is called to order!" Mary announced, nibbling a cookie. She had a real Cabinet—a number of high level advisors—to help her with all her presidential duties and situations. But sometimes, she found her "Kitchen Cabinet" of friends much more helpful.

"So, what's up?" asked J.J., flouncing on the floral-cushioned sofa.

"Yes, Mary, you look sort of worried today," said Mico. "What's going on in the world that has your brow getting little wrinkles? Are we having another war, or something?"

Beah nodded. "You usually text me once a day and I haven't heard from you all weekend. Is there a problem?"

"We can help with problems!" said Kinta.

"It's money," said Mary.

"Oh, don't worry about that," said Mico, reaching in her jeans pocket.

"No, no!" said Mary, waving her hands, as her friend plucked out a $5 bill. "Not that kind of money." The girls looked puzzled.

"Well, what kind of money, then?" asked Mico.

"Embezzled money?" guessed Beah.

"Stolen money?" J.J. speculated.

"That's the same thing," argued Kinta.

Mary held up her hand. "No. It's the kind of money with lots and lots of zeroes at the end of it."

"Thousands?" asked Mico.

"Millions?" suggested Kinta.

"Billions?" wondered J.J.

Mary shook her head slowly. "All of those," she said. "It's the TRILLION dollar U.S. budget that's got me down."

"Wow!" said J.J. "A trillion dollars—that's a LOT."

"That's an understatement!" said Kinta.

"Well, everything's relative," said Mary, squashing herself back into the cushy sofa cushions warmed by sunlight spewing through the sun porch windows.

Kinta threw up her hands. "Well, I sure don't have any relatives with a trillion dollars!"

The girls giggled.

"So what's the problem?" Mico asked. She picked up the pitcher and poured more pink lemonade for everyone.

"The problem is red ink," Mary explained. "And earmarks. And pork barrel spending."

The girls looked at her like she was speaking a foreign language.

"Red ink?"

"Earmarks?"

"Pigs in barrels?"

"What in the world are you talking about, Mary?" Beah asked for them all.

Mary explained: "Well the budget that was presented to me is a lot higher in spending than in what the government gets in taxes. That means the budget is not balanced. So the deficit—the difference—is called red ink. And red ink is a no-no."

"I hear that," said J.J. "You can't spend more than you make my Mom always says."

Mary continued: "And earmarks are when people sneak in special projects to spend money on in the state they come from."

"Well, that's not so bad, is it?" asked Mico. "They are here in Washington to represent the people."

"Some of the things aren't bad," said Mary. "But some are silly, wasteful, or, well, just plain stupid."

"Like what?" asked Kinta.

Mary thought for a moment. "Oh, all kinds of things. Like a study to see which color televisions people like the best. Or to build a road where there aren't really any people living, or going to live there. Or, maybe, I don't know, to invent a better chocolate chip," she said, opening her handful of crumbs for them to see.

"Aw, you can't invent a better chocolate chip!" said J.J.

"A road to nowhere sounds pretty dumb," said Kinta.

"It seems like curing cancer or something would deserve more money that worrying about the color of a television," added Beah.

"So just tell those silly, old Congresspeople that they can't do all that," Mico said.

Mary sighed. "I plan to," she said. "I have to. But I don't want to just veto the budget. I want to give them a better idea of how to balance the budget so I can sign it into law. I have an idea," Mary admitted.

For the next ten minutes Mary told her friends about the idea that had been percolating in the back of her mind all day. "So, you see," she finished, "I really need your help. I have to go to Capitol Hill *tomorrow*."

"Well, we can go with you!" said Kinta. "Remember there's a teacher's workday tomorrow. We'll help you be ready to teach those folks a financial thing or two."

"Gee, Mary," said Beah, patting her friend's freckled hand. "I'm sure glad I don't have your job. The only math I have to worry about is black ink math."

Mary smiled at her friend and picked up the special phone on the table. An aide answered immediately: "Yes, Miss President, how may I help you?" It was then that Mary gave the aide a most unusual order for an odd assortment of special supplies. Nonetheless, the aide never hesitated. "Of course," he said. "Right away!"

Monday, 6:00 p.m.
The Residence

ONCE ALL THE supplies arrived, the girls gathered around the Family Dining Room table, which Ms. Hightower had covered with a large plastic cloth, at Mary's request.

Mary made sure all the doors were closed before they began to unpack the bags of supplies that had arrived promptly, as promised. She told Todd to be sure no one came in while they were at work.

Because tomorrow was a school holiday, Gramps, Aunt Doodah, Josh, and baby Prissy had gone out to eat at a local restaurant for a change. Ms. Hightower had left the girls a large cheese and pepperoni pizza (prepared by Chef) in the center of the table. Mary guessed Ms. Hightower had thought they just didn't want to make a mess. But a mess is just what they were about to make.

The girls "oohed" and "aahed" as the supplies were unpacked. They also unpacked the items from their backpacks that Mary had sent word for them to bring today. Following Mary's instructions, they worked while they ate.

"Uh, I think I glued my slice of pizza to the table," said J.J. after a while.

"Well, I think I ate a sequin!" sputtered Kinta.

"Someone hand me a glue stick," said Mico.

"I think we're about done?" guessed Beah.

The girls, smidgens of tomato sauce on their faces, and blobs of glue and glitter on their hands, sat back.

"Looks great!" said Mary. "I can always count on my Kitchen Cabinet to come to the rescue!"

"Anytime!" cried the girls in unison.

"Why don't we just leave all this for now," said Mary, "and go watch a movie like we usually do. We can pack these up in the morning."

Eagerly, the girls agreed.

Monday, 8:00 p.m.
The Lincoln Bedroom

EVEN THOUGH THEY could go down to the White House movie room to watch a movie, they all preferred to climb in the big bed in the Lincoln Bedroom and watch the movie on a flat screen television that Todd rolled in for them.

Knowing this was the plan, Chef had sent up popcorn, candy, and a pot of hot cocoa with homemade pink marshmallows.

"I wish I had a chef," said Beah, as she snuggled down beneath the covers.

"But your Mom's a great cook," J.J. quickly reminded her.

The girls grew silent. Although Mary never talked about her dead parents, her friends tried to remember she was an orphan, in spite of all the family she had living with her in the White House.

"It's ok," Mary said, reading their thoughts. "I love your Mom's spaghetti. And she makes great birthday cakes."

Kinta piled up as many pillows as possible behind her back. "Is it ok to eat in the Lincoln Bedroom?"

Mico giggled. "Well, I don't think Mr. Lincoln will mind."

The other girls giggled, too, then grew silent.

"We've heard sometimes people see President Lincoln's ghost," whispered Beah.

"Have you ever seen or heard him at night, Mary?"

Mary yawned. "Oh, sure, most every night," she said.

"WHAT???!!" the girls squealed, jumping up and scattering popcorn everywhere.

"Really?" whispered Mico.

Mary laughed. "No, sillies! If the White House has a ghost…or ghosts…I haven't met up with them yet. Someone grab the remote and start the movie."

The "movie," as usual, was really a video of Mary's inauguration. Only now they always skipped over the swearing-in ceremony, and most of the parade up Pennsylvania Avenue, to get to the balls so they could admire themselves and their beautiful dresses: Mico in pink; J.J. in purple; Beah in red; Kinta in white; and Mary in gold. They also argued over which of the ladies looked prettiest and which of the younger men were cutest. But because they'd seen the video so many times, one by one they fell fast asleep.

Little could the girls have known that, indeed, ghosts or goblins would be out and about this night in the White House…and very close by.

Tuesday, 8:00 a.m.
The Lincoln Bedroom

THE BEDROOM WAS dark. The movie had run so long, that instead of going to Mary's bedroom like they usually did, the friends had fallen asleep like a pile of kittens in the big, historic bed.

A light tap on the door awakened them.

"Miss President," called Todd. "This is Capitol Hill day. I guess you are up getting dressed?"

Startled, Mary sat straight up. "Uh, yes, Todd, we are," she said. "Soon."

She shook her sleepy-headed friends and one by one they grumbled and woke up.

"I don't know when I've overslept since I've been President," Mary marveled. She reminded herself not to sleep in the dark, old Lincoln Bedroom ever again.

"But school's out," moaned J.J.

"But Congress is in session!" said Mary. "And I have to be there in one hour. If you're going with me, better rise and shine!"

"I'll rise," Beah said, rubbing her eyes and slipping on her fuzzy pink slippers. "But I won't shine."

As soon as she said "shine," the bedroom door spun open. There stood Gramps in his stripped pj's. His hair stuck out like some ancient

composer or scientist or the guy on the $20 bill. "Mary!" he called. "You'd better come—quick!"

Startled, all Mary's friends could think of was some national emergency. Were they going to have to evacuate the White House? Was Air Force One going to fly them to an undisclosed location—maybe a cave—to live because they were with the President? Was there a war?

Mary was surprised, but calm. She hopped out of bed and put on her robe. It had the Presidential Seal on the back. "Come on," she told her friends. "Follow me. Let's see what's up."

The truth was that Mary might have suspected most anything except what they discovered. Gramps led them parade-style to the swinging door that opened to the Family Kitchen. When he switched on the overhead light, the girls gasped.

"Oh, my gosh!" squealed J.J.

"What happened here?!" cried Beah.

"Disaster! Disaster!" swore Kinta.

"Boy, howdy," said Mico. "Someone's in major trouble."

Mary just stood there and stared. After all their hard work last night, their efforts were an enormous mess. It was clear that someone had sabotaged their work. The items she planned to take to Congress were tipped over left and right. Glitter, and sequins, and streaks of tempera paint were smeared everywhere. Crystals and beads and little pieces of curly wire and more were scattered across the table and the floor.

On the wall, they could see handprints of glue, the palms and fingers glistening with pink and gold and silver and green glitter and sequins.

"Who could have done this?" asked Beah, near tears.

"And why?!" wondered Kinta.

"Maybe it was Lincoln's ghost?" J.J. speculated.

"No!" said Mico, stamping her foot. "But someone very, very bad!"

Suddenly, the door swung open. Todd escorted the three culprits into the room and once more, the girls gasped in shock.

Mary shook her head in dismay. There stood her sleepy brother, Josh, his pajamas a whirlwind of paint and sequins. Toddling toward her was Prissy, her blond curls a mass of crystals. Between Todd's big feet slithered Ssss—who was covered in purple glitter. They were a mess!

"Why did you wake me up?" groused Josh. "I'm not the President. I'm just the pesky, little brother and school's out, so I can sleep in." When he looked at the table, he just added, "Uh, oh." He looked like he might bawl any minute.

"Can you explain, Josh?" Mary asked gently.

"Sssure," Josh said. "We came back from dinner and Gramps went to bed and Aunt Doodah got a phone call. She must have gone to bed because I didn't see her again. We saw all this stuff on the table and it looked like it needed...finishing, so I started on it, and Prissy tried to help me. I don't know when Ssss did his thing. But when we were done, I just took Pris on to bed with me. I, uh, hope we did a good job?"

Gramps just shook his head and wandered off toward the coffee pot.

Todd frowned and went back to his station.

Aunt Doodah was nowhere to be seen.

Ssss curled up in the corner, completely unconcerned about all that had just taken place.

The girls looked like they could cry. Or beat Josh up. Or scream. They looked at Mary.

Mary smiled at Josh. "It's fine, Josh," she surprised the girls by saying. "You did a fine job. Why don't you take Prissy to the sun porch and I'll see you get some cereal and juice. I think Ms. Hightower is off today, but I'm sure Gramps will bring it down. You guys can watch cartoons, ok?"

Her brother looked relieved. "Thanks, sis," he said. He picked up the baby, who now had glitter on her tongue. Just before he left the room, he turned around. "And good luck with that Congress thing today," he added.

His sister bowed her head then looked back up. "Thanks, Josh. You enjoy your day out of school. I'm sure Aunt Doodah and Gramps will take you two to the Mall when they get up and around. I'll see you this afternoon. We'll bowl in the White House bowling alley, ok?"

Josh grinned. "Cool! Thanks, Mary. See ya." He turned and left the room.

The girls stared at Mary.

"Well, I guess we see why you're President…" started Beah.

"…and we're not!" finished J.J.

Mary shrugged her shoulders. "You learn to pick your battles," she said.

"But now what?" asked Kinta. "What about your idea? It's shot all to…sequins, seems to me."

"No problem," said Mary, gently lifting one of the objects up for them to see. "Actually, I think these are absolutely perfect. Let's pack them up, get dressed, and go."

Tuesday, 9:00 a.m.
Pennsylvania Avenue

THE GIRLS HAD dressed quickly, still brushing the occasional sequin or glitter or crystal

from their hair, dresses, or shoes. Todd had packed the "items" in the back of the large, black limousine with the Presidential Seal on the door.

With Mary leading the way, they walked out of the White House beneath the portico and climbed into the car. With the squeal of a police siren ahead, the car sped off down Pennsylvania Avenue toward Capitol Hill.

"This is great fun!" said J.J. "I'd like to have a car like this."

"I want a little red convertible when I grow up," said Kinta.

"I'll have a horse, thanks," said Beah.

"If I had my own taxicab, I could make some money," said Mico. "What about you, Mary?"

But their friend was staring out the window. Sometimes she waved at the excited people lined up along the roadway to see the

President pass by. But mostly she looked thoughtful, and a little worried. And her friends grew quiet.

Tuesday, 9:30 a.m.
The U.S. Capitol

"I'VE SAVED YOU special seats," she promised her friends. "Todd will escort you there."

"So, we'll see you afterwards?" asked J.J.

Mary smiled. "Oh, much sooner than that," she said. "I still need your help."

When the girls looked puzzled, she jiggled her thumb toward the trunk of the car. "I need you to bring the you-know-whats forward when I give you the signal," she said.

"In front of all those people?" Beah asked, nervously. She was pretty shy.

"What if we trip? Or get lost? Or break something?" asked Kinta. "This is Congress, you know."

"Don't worry," Mary said, with a wave of her hand. "Those things happen here all the time. Don't worry. Just watch for my signal."

Suddenly, the car door was opened and Mary was helped out and whisked into the building. Slowly, with goosebumps pimpling their arms and butterflies swarming in their stomachs, her friends followed.

Mary was nowhere to be seen when her friends took their seats. Todd had placed a box beneath each of their chairs and scurried off. A general hubbub of shuffling and voices filled the great hall until the first trumpet sounded:

BAMP PAH BA BAH PAM BA BAH!

BAMP PAH BA BAH PAM BA BAHHHHH!

"LADIES...AND...GENTLEMEN: THE PRESIDENT OF THE UNITED STATES!"

A roar of cheers and applause went up as Mary padded down the red carpet as the tune *Ruffles and Flourishes* filled the hall. Mary was greeted at the podium, where she had to stand on a little step to look over the top of the mass of microphones.

As she stared at the Joint Session of Congress, Mary thought how great America was. The people here represented all the people in all the states. The representatives and senators weren't perfect, but most worked hard to do the best for the state they represented.

During elections, people argued whether Democrats were best, or Republicans, or liberal, or conservative, or this group or that group or this idea or that idea, but really, when it all came down to it, Mary thought, they were all Americans. While some countries duked it out in wars, at least America tried to solve their differences with talking (and, alas, talking and talking and talking), and laws.

That's why Mary hated to come and say "Thanks, but no thanks" about the budget under consideration. But she still thought her idea would work—if no one laughed at her or made fun of her idea, and if they did, well that was just too bad—she trusted her instincts and so she still had to try it.

Soon, they said the Pledge of Allegiance and sang the National Anthem and it was time for Mary to speak. She looked down at her four special friends in the front row. They each gave a wink, a wave, a thumbs-up, or an "ok" sign.

Mary began…

After almost an hour of talking…a lot of applause…some rumbling and grumbling…and a lot of squirming by her friends, Mary concluded:

"So as I have said, I just can't approve this budget. I know you have worked hard on it and I appreciate that. I know the American people do. I know I'm just a kid, but kids have great ideas. I know I'm just a girl, but girls grow up to become the breadwinners for their families. In school we learn that 2 and 2 equal four…and so I propose not only that the budget be balanced before I sign it into law, I offer an idea that I think the American people will understand and approve of."

Mary gave the signal—a brief nod of her head to her friends—and they pulled the boxes from beneath their chairs and marched forward. As they unpacked the items from the cartons, Mary added:

"There is one item for each of you. They have been especially [it was the only time she hesitated], uh, especially designed for your state. Take your item and figure out the amount you need to cut out of your state's part of the budget. Put a slip of paper with that amount on it inside of your item. Return these items to me in one week, and I believe that we will have black ink, not red ink, a balanced budget—one that we all can be proud of. That all Americans can be proud of. Thank you!"

To bewildered stares, Mary came down off the dais and joined her friends, who had their boxes wide open.

"ALABAMA!" shouted J.J., and a puzzled Congresswoman came forward.

"IOWA!" yelled Mico over the din of noise.

"NEW YORK!" cried Kinta.

"CALIFORNIA!" called Beah.

The rest of the states were called and all the items were handed out. Soon the hall was filled with people milling around, talking, some scratching their heads, but all of them holding the items they had been given—PIGGY BANKS! Silver banks, gold banks, red banks, blue banks. Some decorated with glitter and sequins. Others decorated with squiggles of wire, crystals, and beads. All a tad *overdecorated*, thanks to Josh, Prissy, and Ssss, but no one seemed to mind.

Suddenly there was a roar of applause. "MARY! MARY! MARY! MARY!" the people chanted. They held their adorable piggy banks up in the air as they cheered. The television lights caused the beautiful pigs to glisten and glow. The camera crews tried to capture all of the banks, each labeled with the name of one of the 50 states.

"Miss President," a deep voice said, and the girls turned to see Todd. He motioned for them to walk down the aisle, and this time, the girls—the Kitchen Cabinet—followed their friend, their President, close behind.

It was slow going.

"Thank you, Miss President," someone said, stopping Mary to shake her hand.

"Great idea!" called out another person.

"Love it!" said someone else, who shook Beah's hand.

And so their slow parade made it down the aisle with the girls getting cheers, and praise, and handshakes, and pats on the shoulder. One very elderly Congressman near the back of the hall held his pig close and stared at it. By the time Mary got to him, he looked up, tears in his eyes.

"Just like the Great Depression," he said softly to her. Mary was worried about him. "Wonderful idea," he said. "I thought the old days were forgotten, the old ways. No free lunch. Don't spend more than you earn. From the mouths of babes," he added. Then, "Oh, sorry, Miss President, I meant no disrespect."

Mary smiled at the man, then reached up and gave him a little kiss on his pale cheek. "None taken," she said. "Just fill-er-up, please!" He nodded.

Soon they were whisked back in the car, which seemed deadly silent after all the noise and the TV cameras and the shouts of reporters. Until, suddenly, the girls burst into giggles.

"You did it! Mary, you did it!" Kinta squealed.

"It was a great idea!" said Beah, as the car sped them back to the White House.

"Amazing!" said Mico. "So this is how politics works—strange, very strange."

"I'm so proud of you, Mary!" said J.J. "You did it! Girls rule!"

Mary smiled at her friends, but she shook her head No-No-No. "I didn't do it," she said, pointing to each of them—*"WE DID IT!"*

Tuesday, noon
The White House, South Lawn

THE GIRLS WERE still excited when they got back to the White House, but a little disappointed to see their Moms or Dads standing on the South Lawn.

"Aw, I wish we didn't have to go home so soon," J.J. said.

"I want to stay and celebrate Mary's success," said Beah.

"Shucks!" said Mico. "I thought we'd at least get to stay with you the rest of the day."

"Why do our parents have our...sleeping bags?" Kinta asked.

Mary smiled. "Because you're not going home," she said. "You're coming with me to Camp David for the rest of the week! I had Gramps call all your parents while we were at the Capitol. It's all arranged." Mary hesitated. "I mean if you want to go?"

"I don't know," said Mico. "Camping's not my thing, you know. Mosquitoes, big deer, snakes, stuff like that."

"Don't be silly," J.J. told her. "Camp David's not some tooky little Boy Scout camp. It's the Presidential Retreat. Pretty first class, but with lots of outdoor things to do, if you want to."

"How'd you know all that?" asked Kinta, suspiciously. "Have you been there with Mary and we haven't?"

"No!" said J.J. "I read! I read all about Camp David before."

"Well, I sure want to go!" said Beah. She stalked off toward her Mom to get her sleeping bag and say goodbye.

The other girls headed that way, then froze. "Uhhhhh, Marrrry?" they said together, turning to look at their friend.

Mary shrugged. "Sorry," she said, motioning to the Air Force One helicopter, which was revving its engines in preparation for take-off.

Mary pointed to Gramps, Josh, Aunt Doodah, Priscilla, and Ssss, as they walked, crawled, or slithered up the steps and into the

aircraft. "I have a lot of presidential power, but there are some things I can't do anything about." She shrugged her shoulders. "Sorry about the snake," she added to Mico. "But we do have mosquito spray...and s'mores."

"S'MORES!" squealed the girls and they all ran to get their gear and climb aboard the plane.

"Mary," a voice said behind her. Mary turned and there stood Todd. He handed her a large paper grocery sack.

"What's this?" she asked.

Todd winked. "You know: graham crackers, chocolate, marshmallows."

"Oh, gosh, Todd, thanks!" Mary said. "And, by the way..."

"Yes?" Todd said seriously.

Mary grinned and pointed downward. "Uh, you have green glitter all over your shoes!"

As Air Force One's props began to *whirrrrr*, Mary settled into her seat and buckled her seatbelt. She tucked a little red, white, and blue piggy bank she had made for herself into her duffle bag. Out the window, she watched the Mall speed by beneath them in a green blur and the Washington Monument wink its red light at her. She gave Lincoln a little wave as they sped over his monument by the reflecting pool and whispered, "No more popcorn in your bed, I promise!"

The last thing Mary saw before the pilot swooped them toward the mountains and Camp David was the White House receding in the distance. *Home, sweet home*, she thought. *See you Monday.*

BUDGET IS BALANCED! "BLACK INK, NOT RED!" "AMERICANS APPROVE!" CHEERS CONGRESS

CAPITOL HILL: Congress today patted themselves on the back for achieving a balanced budget. "We've worked very, very hard for the American people to pull this off," said Congresswoman Erica Jones.

"It only makes sense to have a balanced budget," said the Congressman from Wyoming. "It's what the American people expect. We just can't operate in red ink. We can't have bills that our children or grandchildren have to pay for later."

Congress congratulated themselves on the completion of the annual chore to get a budget that is acceptable. They noted their many hours, weeks, and months of hard work to achieve their goal. "I think we did a great job," said a number of representatives as they left to return to their home states.

President Mary America signed the budget earlier today and sent congratulations to be read on the Congressional floor. She also sent Congress a large PIGGY BANK cake, prepared by the White House chef.

commander-in-chief

Carole Marsh

About the Author

Carole Marsh is an author and publisher who has written many works of fiction and non-fiction for young readers. She travels throughout the United States and around the world to research her books. In 1979 Carole Marsh was named Communicator of the Year for her corporate communications work with major national and international corporations.

Marsh is the founder and CEO of Gallopade International, established in 1979. Today, Gallopade International is widely recognized as a leading source of educational materials for every state and many countries. Marsh and Gallopade were recipients of the 2004 Teachers' Choice Award. Marsh has written more than 50 Carole Marsh Mysteries™. In 2009, Marsh started the 21st Century Skills Institute to help children better understand what they need to learn to become financially savvy and to secure a good job so that they may grow up and become an effective breadwinner for their family. She works with her own family, husband Bob Longmeyer, daughter Michele Yother, son Michael Longmeyer, and her grandchildren serve as characters in many of her books.

Ms. Marsh welcomes correspondence from her readers. You can e-mail her at fanclub@gallopade.com, visit carolemarshmysteries.com, or write to her in care of Gallopade International, P.O. Box 2779, Peachtree City, Georgia, 30269 USA.

Talk About It...

BUILT IN BOOK CLUB

Questions to Discuss!

1. Would you like to grow up and be President of the United States? Why or why not?

2. How important do you think school studies would be if you ended up serving as President? Which classes or subjects might be especially important, and why?

3. How do you think Mary feels about being President? What do you think are her favorite parts of the job? Her least favorite parts?

4. What emotions do you think Mary might feel as she does her job? (Busy, lonesome, nervous, frustrated, happy, sad, proud, etc.)

5. How do you think Mary's family in the White House helps and supports her?

6. What do Mary's "Kitchen Cabinet" of friends mean to her?

7. How did Mary work out her problem of getting Congress to balance the budget?

8. What do you think are important attitudes and attributes to have as President? Does Mary have these?

9. What do you think are the most important requirements for being President—honesty, integrity, age, gender, intelligence, etc.?

10. What do you think Mary might do/encounter next in her job as President?

Bring it to life...

BUILT IN BOOK CLUB

Activities to do!

1. Make your own "piggy bank!" Find a box, jar or any type of container. Decorate it in your own style using markers, glitter, stickers, or other decorations. Be sure you remember to cut a slot in the top for you to place your money inside!

2. Mary America has many responsibilities as the President of the United States. Make a timeline of what you think a president's typical day is like. Some ideas to get you started are: meetings with Congressmen and Congresswomen, travel to foreign countries, bowling in the White House bowling alley! (Presidents can have fun too!)

3. Mary's pet snake Ssss lives with her in the White House. Make a matching game of previous U.S. Presidents and the names of their presidential pets! For example, President Barack Obama and his dog, Bo!

4. Draw a map of the inside of the White House as you envision it! Be sure to include the Oval Office, the West Wing, the Lincoln Bedroom, the State Ballrooms, and of course the White House movie theater!

5. Create your own Kitchen Cabinet of advisors! Pick friends or classmates to be the members. Assign each member a title and responsibility that suits their skills—like "Secretary of Basketball" or "Secretary of Fashion!" Call the meeting to order, and have each member brief you about their position!

Glossary

Adam Smith: a man who wrote a famous book about money

capital: a place; Washington, DC is the capital of the United States

capitol: a building; Congress meets in the Capitol Building

commander-in-chief: the person in charge of the armed forces, or military, of a country

Congress: the joint leadership (of state senators and state representatives) that conduct the business of the people of the United States

dais: (day es) a platform, usually at the front of a hall, where someone stands to speak to a group

economics: all subjects related to money

eligibility: meeting certain requirements, such as for a job

Great Depression: A period of American history after the Stock Market Crash of 1929, when many people were out of work for a long time

IQ: Intelligence Quotient; a measure of how smart a person is

"Kitchen Cabinet": an informal nickname for the President's cabinet members or advisors

portico: a covered driveway

"situation": in government talk, this is a "problem" — usually a serious international problem to try to solve through diplomacy (talking)

veto: when the president turns down or "vetoes" a bill

Next In Line!

If the President of the United States dies, resigns, or is removed from office, the Vice President assumes his responsibilities. Congress passed legislation in 1947 and in 1955 to determine the proper succession.

Next in line after the Vice President is:

- Speaker of the House
- President Pro Tempore of the Senate
- Secretary of State
- Secretary of the Treasury
- Secretary of Defense
- Attorney General
- Secretary of the Interior
- Secretary of Agriculture
- Secretary of Commerce
- Secretary of Labor
- Secretary of Health and Human Services
- Secretary of Housing and Urban Development
- Secretary of Transportation
- Secretary of Energy
- Secretary of Education

West Wing Words!

ballot: the piece of paper on which people mark a choice in voting

Cabinet: a group of officials that act as advisors to a head of state

candidate: a person who seeks an office

election: the process of choosing among candidates or issues by voting

governor: the person elected to head a state of the United States

inaugurate: to place, or install, in office with a ceremony

incumbent: the person who currently holds a political office

politics: the way a person believes or thinks in government matters

polls: the place where people go to vote

president: the head of government in a republic (a nation in which voters elect officials to make laws and run government)

resolution: a formal statement by Congress giving its opinion or decision

West Wing: the wing of the White House where the president's office (the Oval Office) and his staff's offices are located

Presidential Firsts!

• **George Washington** was the first president to appear on a U.S. postage stamp, issued in 1847.

• **John Adams** was the first president to live in the White House.

• **Andrew Jackson** was the first president born in a log cabin, in 1767.

• **James Madison** was the first president to regularly wear long trousers (pants) instead of the popular knee breeches.

• **James Monroe** was the first president to ride on a steamship. He rode aboard the *Savannah* in 1819.

• **Herbert Hoover** was the first president to have a telephone in his office.

• **Woodrow Wilson** was the first president to visit a foreign country while in office. He negotiated the peace treaty to end World War I in France in 1918.

• **Franklin D. Roosevelt** was the first and only president to serve four terms in office.

• **Dwight D. Eisenhower** was the first president of all 50 states. Hawaii entered the Union as the 50th state in 1959 during his second term in office.

• **Thomas Jefferson** was the first president to be inaugurated in Washington, D.C. George Washington had been inaugurated in New York, and then in Philadelphia for his second term.

• **Richard Nixon** was the first president to visit all 50 states and was the first president to resign, in 1974.

• **Ronald Reagan** was the first president to appoint a woman to the Supreme Court; he chose Sandra Day O'Connor.

• **Barack Obama** was the first African American to become president of the United States in 2009.

Meet Mary America, Her Family, Kitchen Cabinet Friends, and White House Helpers!

Go to

www.maryamerica.com

Hi, I'm Mary America, age 12, first girl president of the United States!

Please visit my website to learn more about me, meet my sort of wild and crazy family, my fun friends (whom I just couldn't do without!), and my helpers in the White House.

As America's president, I care about YOU and your opinions. So come to the website and email me so we can be friends, too. After all, I really work for YOU, you know!

On the website, you'll meet:

The First Family!

Josh, the First Brother, sort of a pesky one but I love him dearly!

Gramps, my grandfather, the First Gramps. He's my rock and I can always count on him for anything!

Aunt Doodah. She's my ditzy aunt who lives with us. Sometimes, she drives me crazy, but she is really a sweetheart.

Prissy, Aunt Doodah's sweet adorable baby and my niece. She is just too cute, but also a handful since she's crawling and walking!

Ssss, my pet boa constrictor. Don't be afraid! He's a sweetheart, too!

My "Kitchen Cabinet" Friends!

Mico, age 10,
attends Sidwell
Friends School;
wants to be a
doctor!

J.J., age 11, loves
to play soccer!

Beah, age 12,
home schools,
spelling bee star!

Kinta, age 12,
great at math!

My White House Helpers!

Well, some help and some are a thorn in my side, but it goes with the job!

Mrs. Denim, my former fourth grade teacher; now, Secretary to the President of the United States.

The COS, my Chief-of-Staff.

Chef, my White House chef who prepares my family's food as well as state dinners and special snacks for my friends and me.

Todd, my personal Secret Service agent and best White House friend.

Ms. Tendril, my home school at the White House teacher.

Ms. Hightower, takes care of the "Residence" part of the White House where my family and I live.

Enjoy this exciting excerpt from Book 2...

Mary America

First Girl President of the United States

Leader of the free world, commander-in-chief, and handling a crisis in the Situation Room... with the help of her friends!

MARY AMERICA HAD been in office for about a year. She was now fairly accustomed to the routine of being the President of the United States. Everyday was pretty much busy, busy, busy. Between her endless presidential duties, keeping up with her family, home school studies, and trying to make time for her "Kitchen Cabinet" friends, Mary had little time to herself.

As she had begun to think of it, everyday was just another fiddle-dee-dee day full of presidential chores. And this week seemed especially gnarly. The First Gramps, her grandfather, was in the hospital having a pacemaker put in to regulate his heartbeat. He was getting older and Mary worried about him. After all, she and Josh had already lost one grandfather to a heart attack, as well as their mother and father in a terrible bombing accident.

Her little brother Josh had measles of all things! Since they were not sure if he had been vaccinated or not, it was not such a surprise. But he should have had his immunization a long time ago. Still, if their mother and father had been halfway around the world on their jobs, maybe not? He was covered in red spots, and pretty darn cranky. Mary didn't blame him.

Their crazy Aunt Doodah had gone on an impromptu "vacation" and left her baby, crawling/toddling Prissy with a "friend" who had failed to show up, and so Ms. Denim, Mary's Presidential Secretary, was trying to take care of her, in addition to a gazillion other duties. When she was busy, she called on Todd, Mary's Secret Service agent, and Todd was definitely not in a good mood over that unexpected new duty!

It was summer and hot and tempers were high around the world. Mary felt like she was sitting in a hot seat on top of that world. And to make matters worse for the leader of the free world and the commander-in-

chief, Mary had just gotten word that there was a "situation."

Before coming to the White House she thought a situation was a kind of comedy show on television. But a "situation" in the White House meant a crisis, perhaps an earth-shaking, world-changing, life or death crisis.

Mary didn't know what the crisis was yet, but she knew two things:

1. It would be her job to fix it, maybe fast!
2. She would need to depend on her "Kitchen Cabinet" of girl friends to help her through this troubling time.

"I am sure glad they are on their way over this afternoon when they get out of school," Mary said out loud to reassure herself.

"Ms. Denim?" she called to her former teacher, now her Presidential Secretary.

"Yes?" Ms. Denim called from her office, afraid to leave Prissy alone for even one second since as she said, "That baby can get into more trouble faster than the Senator from the Great State of Virginia!"

"I'm heading to the situation room," said Mary. "Please call and check on Gramps and make sure Chef gives Josh tomato soup and grilled cheese for lunch."

"Are you going to eat?" Ms. Denim asked, always worried that Mary was so busy taking care of her family

and the nation that she was not taking good enough care of herself.

"I will," Mary promised, with her fingers crossed. "Just as soon as I get out of the Situation Room and go to class."

Before Ms. Denim could answer, Mary's personal Secret Service agent, Todd, appeared to escort her to the Situation Room in the White House basement.

Mary stood up to leave, tripped, and landed face first in the stack of papers on her Oval Office desk.

"Ssss?" asked Todd.

Mary looked down at her tangled shoelaces. "Ssss," she said. Her pet boa constrictor had twisted her laces together yet again. It was his favorite thing to do—well, outside of scaring Ms. Hightower, the First Family's caretaker in the Residence on the second floor.

Mary tied her shoelaces and followed Todd out of one of the Oval Office's secret panel doors. As she passed into the hallway and headed toward the basement she mumbled to herself, "Fiddle-dee-dee, what a day indeed! Can it possibly get worse?"

It could...and it would.

Book 3...

MARY AMERICA

First Girl President of the United States

War and peace, red tape, funny money, Air Force One...and Disney World diplomacy!

Join Mary America and her "Kitchen Cabinet" girl friends as they face-off against some cantankerous world leaders, unearth some counterfeit big bucks, cut a load of red tape all to pieces, and otherwise have a blast (off?!) as Mary conducts her presidential duties with pizzazz and fun!

INTERVIEW WITH THE CREATOR OF...

Carole Marsh

Interviewer: Ms. Marsh, at this point in your 30 year career of writing fiction and non-fiction for children, what made you decide to create a First Girl series?

Author: As a child I developed a great appreciation for how women, such as my mother, who came of age in the 1940s, were still closer to the era of fewer rather than more choices. I thought of it as past Women's Suffrage, but still Women's Suffering, and less the Feminine Mystique and more the Feminine Miss-out on a lot of things that they were smart enough for, but not invited or welcome to the party. Even when I was entering business 30 years ago, it was still somewhat iffy about what women could not do. I found it frustrating to be considered "too young" for some things, as if age versus talent and determination had anything to do with competitive success. Also, for women, first you were too young (or too something!), then you were too old. There just seemed to be too many rules because we were girls. The logic of that completely eluded me. This constant background noise bugged me to always keep girls equal or at the forefront of my

writing. I think all of a sudden I felt I'd never be satisfied until I gave girls a few "promotions" along the way!

Interviewer: As in first female president of the United States?

Author: Exactly! And more cool "top jobs" in future books in this series, which will be a trilogy of titles about 3 different girls, nine books in all, someone any girl can identify with.

Interviewer: And all of these are your alter egos?

Author: (laughs) Almost certainly!

Interviewer: Was there any time in your past where you really felt the pinch of let's call it bias against women's abilities?

Author: In the late 1970s, I believe, I wrote a full-page newspaper feature about the issue of a young men's organization's fight over whether or not to accept women into their organization. Their theme was "Young Men Can Change the World." My article started out: *Young women can change the diapers, the sheets, their clothes, and their minds—but can they change the world?* Actually, it was a very unbiased article filled with quotes from members on both sides of the question. But it sure created a local hullabaloo! I was so surprised. It did not matter to me if this organization remained all men or not, especially, but they sure looked bad to vehemently (at that time) make it sound like women were what?—unable to help change the world except for baking cakes for fundraisers? It just made me aware that while on the surface it can appear a bias has receded, if not completely vanished, it can lurk just under the skin with real repercussions for women, of commission, or of omission.

Interviewer: Since you are an entrepreneur and business owner, do you ever feel you've been the target of such bias in the business world, meaning that more subtle, behind-closed-doors type of exclusion from opportunity?

Author: Certainly! I came along businesswise at an age where many men in positions to do so, such as bankers and others, were much more open and fair, but there were still limitations. I had a daughter and I did not want her to feel any limitations. I solved much of this for myself by going into business for myself. Competition's tough enough without having to compete with something you can't help, such as being a woman, especially when you consider that an asset!

Interviewer: And so this was the impetus for Mary America, First Girl President of the United States?

Author: (laughing) Not really! It was underlying, perhaps. But the real impetus was just to do a great read for girls in this age range, to introduce a character to them that I think is a lot like them. Girls may be young, and silly, and giggly, but I know they also think very serious thoughts, have often overcome or are struggling with serious obstacles, and want to grow up and, if not change the world, be the best that they can be. Also, I realized about a year after I wrote the first draft of this book that I was much more bummed out about some current events than I realized, and a lot of that angst had to do with girls, including my grandchildren.

Interviewer: And what current events were those?

Author: Obviously the Enron fiasco, the Wall Street shenanigans, the ridiculous thing where banks did bad then got rewarded with a bailout, and as I continued to write, ever more big government boo-boos, the endless war, and then those dadgum tar balls! It just got my psyche goat and wouldn't let go, although I didn't really realize it at the time.

Interviewer: How so?

Author: In a regular run-of-the-mill year of world messes, I think I would have written Mary as a much sillier character. But I write for kids all the time and have every respect for them. You'd be surprised how hard children's writers have to work to maintain this respect when there are some demands for, let's call it, adjusted, tweaked, or realigned kid's books that reflect certain kinds of agendas. There is no way I would write a book for girls that point blank says how I feel about the issues I just mentioned...my job is to give kids the facts and let them draw their own conclusions. But kids are smart and they can see that things are not right. They hear the news or see headlines: *Are We a Nation of Laws?* and such. I don't want to give them an agenda, I want to give them power. Belief that things can be better. And certain knowledge that they very well might be the answer to a better world. Let's hope so!

Interviewer: You sound pretty political?

Author: Not at all! I always say that I'm just a fourth-grader forever! I try to broach any subject with a fresh eye as if I had just encountered it the first time, as my readers generally are. One of my favorite compliments (and Gallopade, the publisher, gets plenty of them!) is that our books are so unbiased and have no

hidden agenda. I'm not projecting my opinions…I'm trying to help girls gain and protect their own opinions, and be willing to change their minds as they have more information, if that warrants. We talk about critical thinking skills for kids and this is a big one, one that adults often flunk!

Interviewer: And so there's more to Mary America than meets the eye?

Author: There is! So much more than I realized when I first wrote the book. I'm a "cup runneth over" kind of person, so I knew Mary would be very capable as president and be undaunted by anything that came her way. But, as they say, "This is the real world." So, Mary soon set me straight that she WAS the president and that she would dictate this story. To girls, it's just a great read, I hope. But because girls are so smart, I know they will feel some of Mary's angst at having all this responsibility (which compounds in future books). Even though she's very smart, she's still a kid working against some considerable foes, who often don't play fair. Also, she has this sort of dysfunctional home situation, something most kids can identify with!

Interviewer: Mary's an orphan, right?

Author: She and her younger brother, Josh, are orphans and they lost great parents of consequence. Mary is acutely aware of that. Their grandfather died in office. And their other grandfather (the First Gramps) is all the family they really have left. Mary has so many responsibilities, both presidential and personal. And (adding insult to injury?) in spite of her high IQ, she still has to go to school each day in the White House. While I loved Mary and was laughing at and with her, I felt so sorry for her.